There are many versions of this classic tale. In the tradition of the storyteller, each one is uniquely different.

— *Jane Belk Moncure*

Library of Congress Cataloging-in-Publication Data

José, Eduard.
  The steadfast tin soldier.

  (A Classic tale)
  Translation of: El soldadito de plomo.
  Summary: After being accidentally launched on a dangerous and terrible voyage, a one-legged soldier finds his way back to his true love — a paper dancing girl.
  [1. Fairy tales.   2. Toys — Fiction]
I. Asensio, Agustí, ill.   II. Moncure, Jane Belk.
III. Andersen, H. C. (Hans Christian), 1805-1875.
Standhaftige tinsoldat.   IV. Title.   V. Series.
PZ8.J747 St   1988   [E]   88-35207
ISBN 0-89565-468-7

© 1988 Parramón Ediciones, S. A.
Printed in Spain by Sirven Gràfic, S. A.
© Alexander Publishers' Marketing
and The Child's World, Inc.: English
edition, 1988.
L.D.: B-44.034-88

H. C. ANDERSEN

The Steadfast Tin Soldier

Illustration: Agustí Asensio
Adaptation: Eduard José

Retold by Jane Belk Moncure

The Child's World, Inc.

Once upon a time, a toy maker made twenty-five tin soldiers out of an old cooking pot. All of the soldiers were exactly alike—all except one. That soldier had only one leg. The toy maker had not had enough tin to finish him. But the soldier stood straight and tall with his musket over his shoulder.

All twenty-five soldiers stood at attention in the window of a toy shop—until one day when they were bought for a little boy's birthday.

"Soldiers!" the boy shouted when he opened the gift. And right away he lined them up in rows in front of his toy castle. "My new soldiers will guard my castle and the princess," he said.

Right in the doorway of the castle the little boy put the princess—a beautiful paper doll. She was wearing a white lace dress with a blue ribbon across her shoulder. She was a ballerina doll. She danced on one leg, with the other leg held high behind her.

When the little tin soldier saw her, he first thought she had only one leg too. "She would be perfect as my wife," he said. "But I am afraid she is too grand for me. She lives in a castle. I have only a toy box for a house. And I share my box with twenty-four other soldiers." So the little toy soldier just smiled at the princess.

That first day, the little tin soldier could hardly wait until night fell. For at nighttime, when all the people were asleep, the toys would be able to move about freely. Then the little tin soldier would have a chance to meet the beautiful ballerina. He hid behind a snuffbox so that he would not be put away for the night with the other tin soldiers.

Finally, the little boy went to bed. Immediately, all the toys came to life. The nutcracker sang a song. The colored pencils drew pictures. The stuffed cat chased the wind-up bird. The toy train chugged all around the room. And the dancing doll danced on one leg and smiled at the little tin soldier.

Just as the clock struck midnight, up popped a jack-in-the-box. He was an angry, mean crow. But he didn't scare the toy soldier one bit.

"Tin soldier," yelled the mean crow, "keep your eyes to yourself—not on the beautiful dancer."

The tin soldier stood straight and tall. He pretended he did not hear the ugly crow's words.

"Ignore *me*, will you?" screeched the crow. "Well, just wait. I'll get you for that."

The very next day, the little boy was playing with his soldiers. He put the tin soldier with one leg in the windowsill. It may have been the evil crow, or possibly just a gust of wind, but suddenly, the little soldier fell headfirst into the street! His bayonet was stuck in the cobblestones.

The little boy went to find him, but it began to rain very hard. The child looked and looked, but he could not find the little tin soldier anywhere.

When the rain finally stopped, two little boys came walking by. "Look!" said one. "It's a little soldier. Let's send him out to sea." The boys made a boat out of newspaper, put the tin soldier in it, and away he sailed. Down he went into a large drain pipe, down, down, under the street.

The soldier was frightened, but he stood steadfast, looking straight ahead with his musket over his shoulder. "If only the ballerina were here, I wouldn't mind the dark," thought the soldier. But then he felt bad about such a wish—this was no place for a lady.

Suddenly, he heard a roaring noise. It was a waterfall! The little boat and the tin soldier rushed over the falls.

Now the little tin soldier found himself sailing down another long pipe. It was dark and the water was high, but the little soldier stood straight and tall.

Then suddenly, he heard the screeching of rats. "Don't let him through," yelled a rat. "He doesn't have a pass to go through the drain!" The rats tried to stop the little soldier, but the fast-moving water carried him quickly away.

As the soldier sailed along, he noticed a light up ahead. This cheered the soldier, for he would be happy to get out of the dark pipe.

But his troubles were far from over. The pipe emptied with a rush into a lake. As the paper boat swirled out of the pipe, it fell apart. The little tin soldier was instantly swallowed by a huge fish.

It was even darker in the fish's belly than it had been in the drain, but the tin soldier did not lose his courage. He stood straight and tall.

After a short time, the big fish began flipping about wildly. "What is happening?" wondered the little tin solder. He did not know that a fisherman had caught the fish and was pulling him ashore.

After some time the little tin soldier saw a flash of bright light. A voice shouted, "Look what I have found inside the fish!"

The fish had been sold at the fish market, and it had been bought by the same little boy's father who had first bought all the tin solders! So the little tin soldier was back in his very own house, with the same little boy, and the same toys.

"What an amazing soldier," said the father, "to have traveled in the belly of a fish!"

"How brave he has been," said the little boy. "I will put him in a place of honor where all the other toys can see him."

In no time at all, the little boy put his one-legged toy soldier back in front of the castle with the lovely paper doll at his side. "I will be happy for the rest of my days!" the little tin soldier said to himself. "I will stand straight and tall and guard the ballerina and the castle."

Then, without warning, the little boy's brother grabbed the tin soldier and kicked him into the fire. There's no way to tell for sure why the boy would do such a cruel thing, but perhaps he was jealous of his brother's wonderful toy.

The tin soldier felt terribly hot and began to melt. Still he remained brave, with his musket over his shoulder. He looked at the little doll and she looked at him.

Suddenly, *swish*! A wind gust caught the little dancer and blew her straight into the fire beside the soldier. At last they were together. The fire blazed on in the stove late into the night.

Now that was the end of the steadfast tin soldier and the little dancer. Or was it?

Toys never really die. The next day the maid swept the ashes out of the stove. She was amazed to find a little tin heart and a tiny shred of blue ribbon. She picked up the scraps to take them to her friend, the toy maker. Perhaps he would be able to make a new ballerina doll. And maybe he would make another tin soldier—this time with two legs instead of one!